Pirate Stories

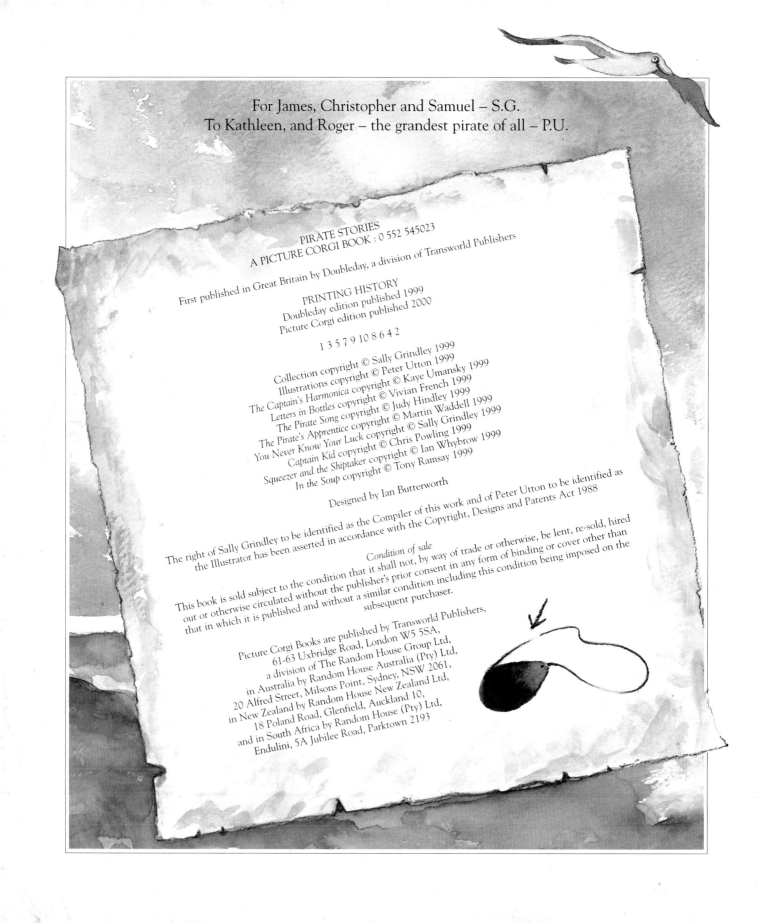

For James, Christopher and Samuel – S.G.
To Kathleen, and Roger – the grandest pirate of all – P.U.

PIRATE STORIES
A PICTURE CORGI BOOK : 0 552 545023

First published in Great Britain by Doubleday, a division of Transworld Publishers

PRINTING HISTORY
Doubleday edition published 1999
Picture Corgi edition published 2000

1 3 5 7 9 10 8 6 4 2

Designed by Ian Butterworth

Picture Corgi Books are published by Transworld Publishers,
61-63 Uxbridge Road, London W5 5SA,
a division of The Random House Group Ltd,
in Australia by Random House Australia (Pty) Ltd,
20 Alfred Street, Milsons Point, Sydney, NSW 2061,
in New Zealand by Random House New Zealand Ltd,
18 Poland Road, Glenfield, Auckland 10,
and in South Africa by Random House (Pty) Ltd,
Endulini, 5A Jubilee Road, Parktown 2193

Pirate Stories

Collected by Sally Grindley
Illustrated by Peter Utton

PICTURE CORGI BOOKS

CONTENTS

THE CAPTAIN'S HARMONICA
by Kaye Umansky

Captain Thunder lay in his hammock blowing on his new harmonica. It was a beautiful night. The ship lay anchored off the coast of a tropical island. A full moon shone on the still sea. There was a balmy breeze blowing, laden with the scent of coconuts. There was no sound...

Except for the Captain's harmonica.

It was a birthday present from his Aunty Maureen. It was shiny silver. It came in a little box, lined with velvet. The moment he saw it, he loved it. The only trouble was, he couldn't play it.

On the far side of the deck, the crew huddled behind a canon. Everyone had their fingers in their ears, apart from the Cook, who had his filled with mashed potato.

"I can't stand it no more," wailed the Bosun. "It's driving me crazy. Sounds like cats fightin' in a sack."

9

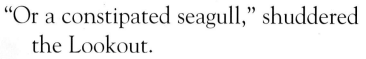

"Or a constipated seagull," shuddered the Lookout.

"A whale with toothache," contributed the Cook.

"Stampeding sea-cows," moaned the Cabin Boy.

"A hippopotamus with asthma, who's just run home through a thunderstorm and finds his dinner isn't ready," suggested the First Mate inventively. He had been good at Creative Writing at school.

"Anyway," said the Bosun.

"Anyway, I can't stand it no more. Come on. We gotter tell him."

And, determinedly, they approached the Captain's hammock.

"Evening, lads," said the Captain, genially. "Listen. I'm really getting the hang of it now."

Everyone winced as he blew a series of hideously clashing discords. The ship's cat fled the deck with its hair on end and hid under the Bosun's bed.

"Recognize it?" said the Captain, coming to an end. "That was *A Life on the Ocean Wave*. Don't go away. I'm going to do *The Drunken Sailor* now."

The Cabin Boy poked the Mate, who nudged the Cook, who elbowed the Lookout, who coughed suggestively at the Bosun. The Bosun stepped forward.

"Us can't stand it, Cap'n," he said. "It's doin' our heads in. Night after night of that there - caterwaulin'."

"I'm sorry," said Captain Thunder with a frown. "Are you referring to my playing?"

"Aye," said the Bosun. "Me an' the boys is all agreed. Either the mouth organ goes or you do."

"Not a chance," declared the Captain stoutly. "I promised Aunty I'd practise every day for a year. Practice makes perfect, you know. I'm staying put and so is my harmonica. And that's final."

A short while later, the Captain found himself standing on a beach, watching in dismay as the crew prepared to depart in their rowing boat.

"This is an outrage!" he bellowed. "How dare you maroon your own Captain!"

"It's not for ever," the Bosun told him kindly. "We'll come back in a year. On your birthday. We've left you a keg of rum and some ship's biscuits and a change of socks."

"And you'll have plenty of time to practise your harmonica," said the Mate. "You should be really good by then."

And they rowed away.

After the initial shock, the Captain found that he rather liked living on the island. He found a freshwater spring, and there were wild yams and coconuts to eat. He caught fish and had little barbecues. He built himself a palm-leaf hut and constructed a comfortable hammock out of vines, which he lay in every night, practising his harmonica.

That's when the trouble with the monkeys began. They didn't like their peace being shattered. They came from all over the island to register their disapproval. They hung in the treetops above him, jeering loudly and pelting him with coconuts.

But the Captain persevered. Night after night he lay swinging gently to and fro, sucking and blowing for all he was worth, ignoring the cross screeching and the sound of coconuts exploding all around him.

And, slowly - because practice does make perfect - he got better. He mastered *I Saw Three Ships*. Then he moved on to *Yes, We Have No Bananas*.

At this point, the monkeys stopped throwing coconuts and began to take an interest. Soon he had *Row, Row, Row Your Boat* under his belt. After that, it was no time until he had cracked *Yellow Bird*. When he attempted *The Sailor's Hornpipe* he was gratified to see that his audience were clapping along and flicking their tails in rhythm!

Now, instead of coming along to protest, the monkeys gathered every evening to listen. They seemed to look forward to it! They brought the Captain nuts and juicy pieces of fruit as encouragement. Sometimes, during the really jolly numbers, they swung down out of the trees and danced on the sand. And when the tunes were sad, they put their arms around each other and sighed heavy sighs.

The Captain mastered *When the Saints* and *Ten Green Bottles*. When he finally worked out the difficult chorus of *The Drunken Sailor* and received a hanging monkey ovation, he knew he had made it. He was finally a harmonica player.

At this point, he became a bit lonely. There wasn't any challenge left in his life. He spent long hours sitting on the cliff top looking out to sea, playing the blues while his monkey friends patted his knee sympathetically and tried to feed him bananas.

Then, when a whole year had passed by, it happened! His old ship appeared on the horizon, with the good old Jolly Roger fluttering in the breeze. And there was his crew, rowing towards him and waving merrily. It was a sight that warmed his heart.

The Captain ran gladly down to
the beach with the monkeys
scampering at his heels.

"Hi there, Cap!" shouted the
Bosun. "Happy Birthday! We've
missed you! How's it going?"

"Fine!" yelled the Captain
cheerfully. "Listen to this!"
And he whipped out his harmonica and
played *I've Got a Luvverly Bunch of Coconuts*
faultlessly, from beginning to end.

"Fantastic!" cheered everyone.

"It's amazing what a bit of practice can do," marvelled the Lookout. "In you get, then, Cap'n. We've baked you a birthday-cum-welcome-home cake. And there's a present waiting for you in your cabin. From your Aunty Maureen."

There was, too.
It was an accordion.

LETTERS IN BOTTLES

by Vivian French

Monday

Dear Mum,

I am sorry that I ran away from home, but I didn't want to work in the fish shop. I didn't like the way the fish looked at me. I am going to make my fortune, and when I am RICH I will come home and bring you diamonds and rubies and pearls. I will make my fortune quite soon because I have got a good job. I am a PIRATE! Captain Spiker Block is a nice man and he has promised me I will get VERY RICH INDEED if I work hard. I am cabin boy on board the "Awful Ada". I am very well and I have two pairs of clean socks with me. Also a clean vest. Please could you send me an eye patch? And a cutlass would be useful.

Your loving son,

Joe Jugg

Tuesday
Dear Mum,
      I feel sick. Very.......................

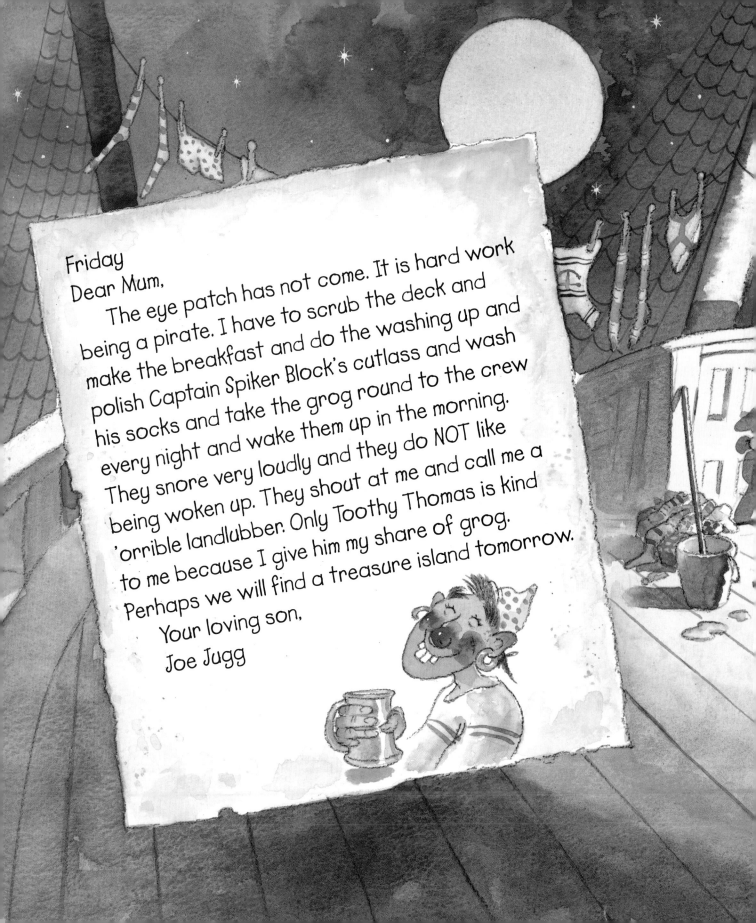

Friday
Dear Mum,
    The eye patch has not come. It is hard work being a pirate. I have to scrub the deck and make the breakfast and do the washing up and polish Captain Spiker Block's cutlass and wash his socks and take the grog round to the crew every night and wake them up in the morning. They snore very loudly and they do NOT like being woken up. They shout at me and call me a 'orrible landlubber. Only Toothy Thomas is kind to me because I give him my share of grog. Perhaps we will find a treasure island tomorrow.
        Your loving son,
        Joe Jugg

Wednesday

Dear Mum,

I am fed up. It is no fun being a pirate, and I want to run away to land. All we do is sail over miles and miles of sea and it all looks just the same.

Today Captain Spiker Block made me eat cold slimy rice pudding for dinner because a rat had made a nest inside his hat. It was a dear little rat, and I have given it one of my socks as a nest. I think I will call him Ratty.

Your loving son,
Joe Jugg

Dear Mum,

I have forgotten what day it is.

This afternoon we saw another ship flying the skull-and-crossbones. Their sails were all tattered and torn, and the ship looked as if it was hardly moving. Captain Spiker Block looked very pleased; he said it was the "Terrible Tara".

"We'll capture her and feed her crew to the sharks!" he said, and he took the wheel to steer the "Awful Ada". All our crew cheered. I was quite excited, although I wished we'd found a treasure island instead.

We chased after the "Terrible Tara", but somehow she slipped away when it got dark. I don't think Captain Spiker is very good at steering. We went round in circles a lot.

In the evening Captain Spiker said everyone could have extra grog, which was odd. I asked why, and he got very, very angry and made me run round and round until I was dizzy. Then he told Toothy Thomas to play his squeeze box while I danced, and he threw tin tacks on the deck so I had to hop and skip and jump while he laughed and laughed and laughed. I had to dance until Toothy went to sleep on top of his squeeze box. I think it was the extra grog that made him so sleepy.

I have decided that Captain Spiker is not at all nice. He is mean and nasty and wicked. Tonight he is being very odd. He is creeping about on deck and he keeps laughing a horrible laugh. Why do you think he is laughing? All the pirates are snoring very VERY loudly so it is very noisy. I can't sleep and I expect I will feel bad in the morning. Ratty has moved into my pocket.

    Your loving son,

    Joe

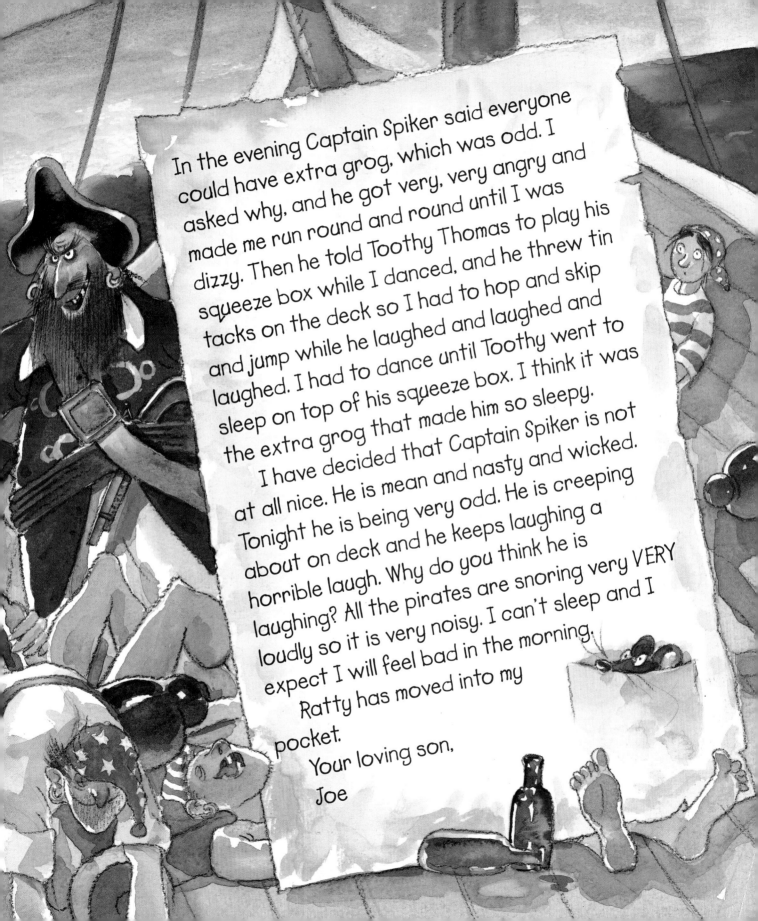

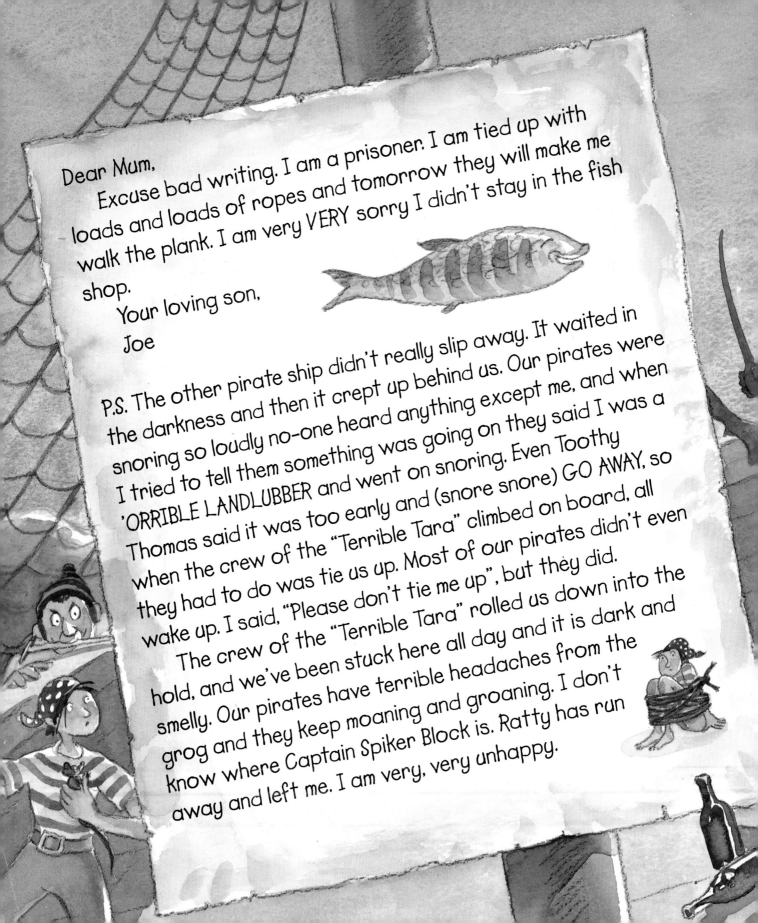

Dear Mum,

Excuse bad writing. I am a prisoner. I am tied up with loads and loads of ropes and tomorrow they will make me walk the plank. I am very VERY sorry I didn't stay in the fish shop.

Your loving son,
Joe

P.S. The other pirate ship didn't really slip away. It waited in the darkness and then it crept up behind us. Our pirates were snoring so loudly no-one heard anything except me, and when I tried to tell them something was going on they said I was a 'ORRIBLE LANDLUBBER and went on snoring. Even Toothy Thomas said it was too early and (snore snore) GO AWAY, so when the crew of the "Terrible Tara" climbed on board, all they had to do was tie us up. Most of our pirates didn't even wake up. I said, "Please don't tie me up", but they did.

The crew of the "Terrible Tara" rolled us down into the hold, and we've been stuck here all day and it is dark and smelly. Our pirates have terrible headaches from the grog and they keep moaning and groaning. I don't know where Captain Spiker Block is. Ratty has run away and left me. I am very, very unhappy.

Dear Mum,
      Guess what?
      Ratty hadn't run away. He came
creeping back and he chewed and
chewed until my ropes were undone!
Then I crept over to Toothy Thomas and I
undid his ropes and he said I was a real old sea dog. I
tiptoed up to the hatch to see what was happening on
deck, and THERE WAS CAPTAIN SPIKER BLOCK SWILLING
GROG AND LAUGHING WITH THE CAPTAIN OF THE
"TERRIBLE TARA"!!!!!!!!
      I went to get Toothy, and we listened and
watched . . . and we saw the captain of the "Terrible
Tara" give Captain Spiker Block a HUGE bag of gold
pieces. I asked Toothy what was happening, and
Toothy said * * * * * * * * * * * *!!!!! which was not very
polite even if we HAD been tied up. Then Toothy said
that Captain Spiker Block must have planned for us to
get caught. He said that was why we had been given
extra grog!!!! It was to make us sleepy, and Toothy
said I was a REAL HERO because I had stayed awake!!
      Toothy suddenly said Shhh! and he listened some
more... and then he said * * * * * * * * * * * *!!! AGAIN!!!!

30

I said, "What is it? What is it?" And Toothy told me Captain Spiker was SELLING us! He was selling us to the captain of the "Terrible Tara", and the captain of the "Terrible Tara" was going to

PTO

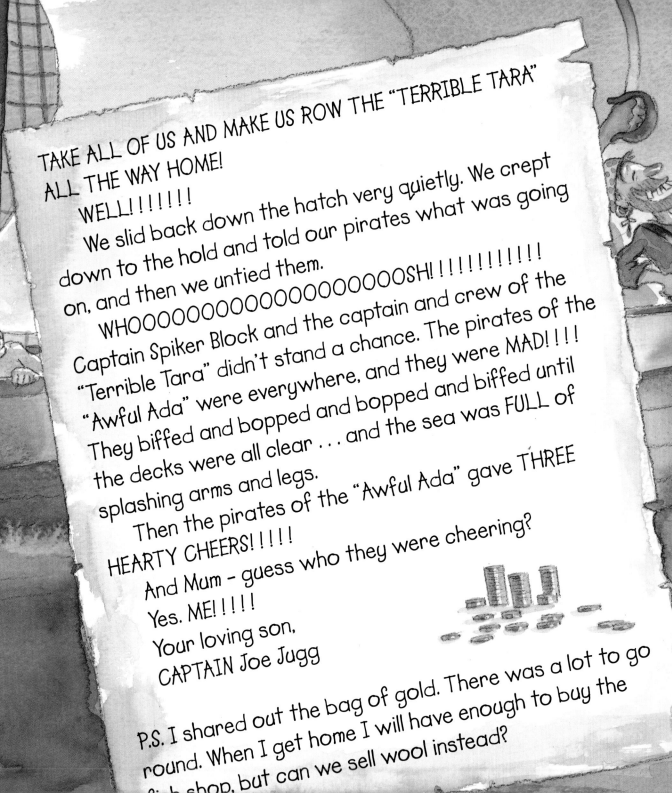

TAKE ALL OF US AND MAKE US ROW THE "TERRIBLE TARA" ALL THE WAY HOME!

WELL! ! ! ! ! !

We slid back down the hatch very quietly. We crept down to the hold and told our pirates what was going on, and then we untied them.

WHOOOOOOOOOOOOOOOOOOOOOSH! ! ! ! ! ! ! ! ! ! ! Captain Spiker Block and the captain and crew of the "Terrible Tara" didn't stand a chance. The pirates of the "Awful Ada" were everywhere, and they were MAD! ! ! ! They biffed and bopped and bopped and biffed until the decks were all clear . . . and the sea was FULL of splashing arms and legs.

Then the pirates of the "Awful Ada" gave THREE HEARTY CHEERS! ! ! ! !

And Mum – guess who they were cheering?

Yes. ME! ! ! ! !

Your loving son,
CAPTAIN Joe Jugg

P.S. I shared out the bag of gold. There was a lot to go round. When I get home I will have enough to buy the fish shop, but can we sell wool instead?

P.P.S. We gave Ratty three cheers as well. And we gave him Spiker Block's hat to live in. Spiker won't need it . . . he was swimming VERY VERY fast when I last saw him, and I THINK it was a shark just behind him . . .

THE PIRATE SONG

by Judy Hindley

I thought I saw a pirate ship,
Riding the ocean blue.
It looked so free and lively,
How I wished to join the crew!

I saw them scamper monkey-like,
Barefoot up the mast -
I saw them set the shining sails
And raise the pirate flag, ahoy!
They raised the pirate flag!

I smelled the salty breezes,
I heard the sails go *snap!*
I saw a name - *The Fancy Nan* -
I wished that I could follow them,
Over the seas and back!

One had a whistling, warbling pipe,
And one of them had a drum,
And one had a wonderful mynah bird
That screeched upon his thumb:
"Come away, then! Come!
Come away with us!"

And all of them danced the hornpipe,
And one and all, they sang:
"We are bad, bad, bad,
We are wicked as can be,
But it's fun, fun, fun
To be so bad!"

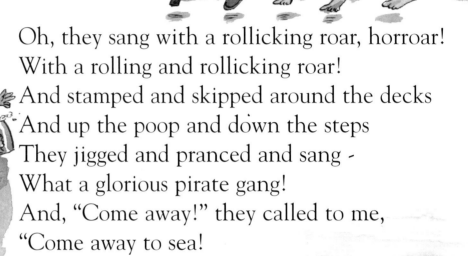

Oh, they sang with a rollicking roar, horroar!
With a rolling and rollicking roar!
And stamped and skipped around the decks
And up the poop and down the steps
They jigged and pranced and sang -
What a glorious pirate gang!
And, "Come away!" they called to me,
"Come away to sea!

"For all we love is treasure trove
And all we do is hunt it -
Up and down the sudsy seas,
Forever we seek for treasure ships,
For all we love is glittery bits,
And all we have is fights and fun,
And all we do is hunt and thieve,
And all we are is bad!"

And then they sang the song again,
As round the decks they ran:
"We are bad, bad, bad!
We are wicked as can be -
But it's fun, fun, fun,
To be so bad!"

Oh, didn't they sing and call to me,
"Come along, then! Come!"
And yet I couldn't do it, quite -
I thought of Dad, and Mum...
And while I watched and wavered
Beside that pirate bark,
The night was softly thickening,
Till all the sea was dark.

And all the while I dithered,
The gathering darkness grew...
Until, behold! - Another ship,
Came swinging into view,
A wonderful strange and ghosty ship -
A ship without a crew!

The ghosty ship was full of gold -
Great heaps of gold doubloons.
Under the rising moon it shone,
Bright as another moon,
But though it sailed so free and fast,
Right smack against *The Fancy Nan* -
So bright and bold, so fast and free -
It didn't make a sound!

"Avast! Belay!" the lookout cried,
As the ghosty ship drew near;
But ever and on, the pirate crew
Kept up their dance and drank their brew,
As though the ship was just a dream
They couldn't see or hear.

There on the deck they'd built a fire,
Round which they marched and sang:
"Come along, then! Come!
Come on and join the fun!"

BUT NOW!
A GHOSTY CREW ROSE UP
AND JOINED THEM
IN THEIR DANCE!

The ghosty crew, they hopped across,
Over the bobbling waves,
And as they hopped, each one of them brought
Great heaps of treasure trove -
Stacks of it and sacks of it,
Doubloons and Louis d'Or -
Enough to fill the pirate ship,
To fill it up
And more.

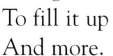

"Avast, belay!" the lookout cried.
The ship began to sink.
And soon, alas, *The Fancy Nan*
Went wallowing into the drink.
And yet, although she sank so low
(And ever the waves rose higher)
As in a trance, the pirate dance
Continued round the fire.

And ever the pirates sang their song,
As though 'twas in their sleep.
They jigged and pranced,
As-lo!-they sank
Straight to the salty deep.

I rubbed my eyes.
The ships had gone.
The night was nearly done.
And all that noisy pirate gang
That sang aboard *The Fancy Nan*,
Had vanished in the early, pearly dawn...
Had simply, sheerly vanished,
In the dawn...

Glunk, glunk,
Glubble,
Blubble,
Gone.

And yet, I seemed to hear them sing
From far beneath the waves,
Till the bubbles up their nostrils
Made them stop:

"We are bad, bad, bad,
We are wicked as can be!
We are -

Glup.
Glup.
Glubble, Bubble,
Glop.

THE PIRATE'S APPRENTICE

by Martin Waddell

PIRATE INDENTURE

This indenture witnesseth that Amy McFee, Pirate Queen, does hereby engage Miss Bad Bertha Smallkid under the terms of the Pirate Trade Regulations (Training) Act 1783 until such time as the said Bad Bertha Smallkid shall satisfy the Examiners-in-Piracy (Apprentice Section) that she has acquired a compentency in her tasks as Pirate outlined in the schedule below.

SCHEDULE
A Saying Rude Words
B Mean Fighting
C Treasure Hunting
D Parrot Care
E Eating mouldy ship's biscuit without complaint
F Such other rough stuff as the said Amy McFee
   may deem necessary

SIGNED   A. McFee (Pirate Queen)
SIGNED   B.B. Smallkid (Aged 6)

It was Bad Bertha's first day on board the *Sea Witch*, with Head Mistress Miss Amy McFee. "Rude Words is the class for today!" said Miss Amy McFee.

The whole pirate class started cursing.

"Oh bother-me!"   "Silly socks!"   "What-a-to-do!"

"That's not Rude Words and Curses!" said Miss Amy McFee, and she taught them some good ones.

"Bare bums!" and "Knickers!" said Miss Amy McFee, and the whole class shouted out "Bare bums and knickers!".

All except Bertha. Bertha was badder. She shouted "✳✳✳✳✳✳" and everyone went red and said, "Shush, Bertha dear."

"Well done, Bertha," beamed Miss Amy McFee. "Go to the top of the class!"

(I know what she said. It was so rude that I can't put it in this book.)

Bad Bertha's next day at school was the one where everyone fought everyone else.

Biff Bang Smash Wallop!

The winner was Bad Bertha Smallkid, black belt, four knock-outs, three falls, one retired hurt, one submission... but she didn't fight fair. She kicked and she tripped and she hit everyone else when they were down. That's because Bertha *was* bad.

"Good Pirate Stuff, Bertha!" drawled Amy McFee.

"Day three! Treasure Day!" said Miss Amy McFee.
They hunted all over the *Sea Witch* for the treasure Miss Amy
McFee and her pirates had hidden: jewels, diamonds and gold.

Bad Bertha found most of the treasure. She would.

She cheated, of course. She sneaked out and looked when
Miss Amy McFee was hiding the treasure,
though she told everyone that she hadn't.

Miss Amy said that didn't matter one bit.
All pirates tell lies and cheat. Cheating and
lying is what pirates do.

"Day four, Parrot Care," said Miss Amy McFee. "First catch your parrot!"

They all ran on shore and caught parrots. Bertha nipped into a store and she bought a stuffed one instead, with some doubloons she'd stolen from Amy McFee's treasure chest.

"Now teach your parrot to talk!" said Miss Amy McFee.

All the good kids taught their parrots nice words like "Pretty Polly" and "Oh What A Nice Boy I Am".

Bertha did it again! She'd popped a small tape player inside her stuffed parrot, with a cassette she'd recorded some days before.

46

The result was her parrot said, "Barebum and knickers," sounding just like Miss Amy McFee.

Miss Amy McFee blushed red with pleasure and pride and Bertha came top of the class. She said that Bertha was the best cheater she knew!

"It is Eating Mouldy Biscuits Class today!" said Miss Amy McFee, the next morning.

You don't want to know what was in the ship's biscuits they ate. Just look:

The squirmy little things are worms. The hairy ones are weevils. I don't know what the other sluggy ones are, and neither did Miss Amy McFee and her pirates. They just closed their eyes and ate most of the time. It was a tough old life, being a pirate.

Most of the class were sick over the side but Bad Bertha wasn't.

Bad Bertha cheated again. She gave all her biscuits away to the other kids' parrots, and the parrots were all sick on the other kids. The other kids had the parrots on their shoulders so they couldn't miss, that's why.

Miss Amy McFee was very impressed, and so was her parrot, Peg Leg.

Rough Stuff was the last day of the course. Rough Stuff thought up by Miss Amy McFee, like...

de-nitting her pirates' beards and

walking the plank for beginners and

swabbing the decks and

cheating at cards and

scuba-diving with rocks round the neck. (Not many survived).

Best of them all was... Bad Bertha. She had big muscles for a very small person and a foul temper and she got most of the others to do her stuff for her... but then pirates are bullies, like Bertha.

"Bad Bertha Smallkid has passed with dishonour!" cried Miss Amy McFee. Bad Bertha went up and got her diploma.

That made her a proper pirate. So she did what pirates do. She was bad. She smash-banged Miss Amy McFee and her crew and cast them away in a small rowing boat with no biscuits. Then she sailed away with Miss Amy's best gold, and all the really bad kids from the class, and Peg Leg the parrot to boot.

Now Bad Bertha is Queen of the Pirates, in place of Miss Amy McFee. Amy McFee sometimes forgot to be bad and was good (well on Christmas Eve, anyway, in the hope of getting presents from the Pirate Santa Claus), and Bad Bertha is bad all the time as a Queen of the Pirates should be... that's why she wound up as the bad Pirate Queen.

The moral is this...

If you are out in a boat and you see a big Pirate Ship captained by Bad Bertha Smallkid...

YOU'RE DEAD!

YOU NEVER KNOW YOUR LUCK

by Sally Grindley

On a beach, on an island, in the middle of nowhere, four men scrambled silently from a rowing boat. Not far out to sea a sailing ship tossed in the waves. It was too dark to see the skull-and-crossbones flying from the main mast, but it was there all right.

Moonlight pierced the clouds and lit up the face of one of the men. The lower half of his face was covered by a thick, tangled beard. A deep scowl creased his forehead and one eye was hidden by an eye patch. The other eye gleamed wickedly.

"Get to it you boneless, jelly-witted, slobbering slug-a-beds."

Captain Deadeye was not known for his charm.

The other pirates, exhausted though they were from days at sea, dragged the rowing boat onto the beach and collected up their weapons.

Just as dawn was breaking, on a beach on the other side of the island two more men jumped from a rowing boat. Not far out to sea another sailing ship tossed in the waves. The skull-and-cross-bones fluttered from the main mast in the early morning breeze.

The first light of day fell on the face of one of the men. The lower half of his face held a big, toothy smile. Lines of laughter spread out across his forehead and his cheeks. His eyes gleamed excitedly, while a parrot sat on his shoulder nibbling his ear.

"Here we are then, Windrush," Captain Hailstone said to the other man. "Now, you have a rest while I see where we need to go next."

"You have a rest," squawked Peanuts.

Captain Hailstone sat down on the beach and spread out a map. "It's right in the middle of the island. We have to go through thick jungle to reach it."

"Right in the middle," squawked Peanuts, and he flew off.

On the other side of the island, Captain Deadeye kicked his pirates into action.

"Get going you revolting, pea-brained, blubber-bellies."

Pirates Greenhorn, Yellowbelly and Redshanks peered around them through the dim light.

"We're not going into that jungle, are we?" said Pirate Yellowbelly.

"That's exactly where we're going," said Captain Deadeye.

"But there might be snakes in there," said Pirate Yellowbelly.

"There might be crocodiles," said Captain Deadeye, "but we're still going in, and you're going first."

"*There might be crocodiles*," squawked a voice. Captain Deadeye glared at his pirates. They looked at each other, amazed that one of them should dare to copy their captain, then headed off into the jungle.

Meanwhile, Captain Hailstone led
Pirate Windrush into the jungle.
Every now and again he stopped to
point out the soldier ants darting
backwards and forwards along the
forest floor or to sniff at a brightly
coloured flower, which he looked up in a
book. He cut down fruit and nuts from the
trees and they feasted as they strode along.

On the other side of the island, Pirate Yellowbelly scrambled through some creeper and stopped in amazement. In front of him was the biggest flower he had ever seen. Its maroon warty petals surrounded an enormous bowl-shaped middle.

"Shiver me timbers, look at this!" Pirate Greenhorn ran forward, tripped on a vine root and fell head first into the flower. "AAARGH!" he screamed as sharp spikes pricked his face and hands. Then "YEUUUUCH!" he howled as the revolting stench of the flower found its way up his nostrils. Pirate Redshanks helped him to his feet and fell back in disgust.

"He stinks, Captain."

"Serves him right," said Captain Deadeye. "We're looking for treasure not namby-pamby flowers."

"*Looking for treasure,*" squawked a voice.

"Who's copying me?" growled Captain Deadeye, while the other pirates stood together with their mouths open and their eyes popping.

"N-n-n-not me, sir," they all cried.

"Do it again and you'll feel the point of my cutlass in your backsides. Now move on."

57

Captain Hailstone and Pirate Windrush sat down on a stump to listen to the tree frogs call and watch squirrels squabble among the creepers.

"There are three-toed sloths in this jungle," said Captain Hailstone, studying his book. "They hang upside down in the trees and their fur is covered with green algae."

"Are they dangerous, Captain?" asked Pirate Windrush.

"Oh no," said Captain Hailstone. "They're so slow they couldn't catch a cold."

On the other side of the island, an ear-splitting scream broke through the canopy of trees. Pirate Yellowbelly had stopped in his tracks and was pointing into the bushes.

"We're being watched," he stuttered. "I can see eyes staring at me."

Pirate Greenhorn looked and screamed. "Aaargh, it's horrible! Its head's upside down and it's covered in green fur."

"*Aargh, it's horrible!*" squawked a voice.

Suddenly, an eerie wailing broke out high up in the trees. It rose and fell, rose and fell over and over again.

"I want to go home," cried Pirate Yellowbelly. "This island is haunted."

"*Go home,*" squawked a voice.

Captain Deadeye drew his pistol and pointed it at his men. "No-one's going anywhere except forwards," he snarled. "I've spent years planning this expedition and we're not giving up now."

Captain Hailstone stopped in his tracks.

"Just listen to that," he said to Pirate Windrush. "Those howler monkeys will keep up their singing for minutes on end. And now the gibbons are joining in."

"I reckon it's like paradise, this island," said Pirate Windrush. "Are we nearly at the middle?"

"Not far," said Captain Hailstone. "I can't wait to get there. I've been planning this expedition for years."

A troop of gibbons surrounded Captain Deadeye and his pirates and began to pelt them with rotten fruit and nuts. The pirates jumped and squealed and ran for the bushes.

"Shoot the hooligans!" yelled Captain Deadeye, but before he could pull the trigger one of the gibbons made off with his pistol.

"Have at you!" he screamed, waving his cutlass.

"*Have at you!*" squawked a voice, and even Captain Deadeye fell silent.

Just then, Captain Hailstone and Pirate Windrush broke through a dense tangle of undergrowth and found themselves by a small waterfall, which cascaded into a river dancing with dragonflies.

"This is it!" cried Captain Hailstone. "This is the spot. Right on the banks of this river. Let's get digging, Windrush, then we can have a swim."

Captain Deadeye woke from his stupor.

"What's that noise?" he snarled. The other pirates listened. They could hear scraping and banging and chiselling and digging.

"Go and see what it is, Yellowbelly."

"Me? Why is it always me?"

"Because I say so, you cockle-brained, chicken-livered jellybaby you."

Pirate Yellowbelly scowled at Captain Deadeye when he thought he wasn't watching, then disappeared through the dense undergrowth.

61

When he came back his knees were knocking wildly. "Captain, you're not going to believe this, Captain..."

PirateYellowbelly told him what he had seen and Captain Deadeye blew his top.

"What! Someone else is digging up MY treasure? Over my dead body!"

"*Over my dead body!*" squawked a voice.

Captain Deadeye drew out his cutlass and charged through the undergrowth like a raging bull. His pirate crew stumbled behind him like headless chickens. He reached the clearing by the river just as Captain Hailstone lifted something above his head and shouted triumphantly, "I've found it!"

"And I'm having it!" yelled Captain Deadeye. "I haven't spent years hunting for this treasure to have it stolen from under my nose by some pot-bellied, pickle-brained land-rat. Hand it over!"

He waved his cutlass menacingly above his head and advanced on Captain Hailstone.

He didn't see the long, lumpy shape slither silently from the water and creep up behind him. Pirate Greenhorn saw it and yelped. The crocodile's mouth opened. Pirate Yellowbelly started to run away.

Captain Hailstone pointed and yelled, "Look out, behind you–" But Captain Deadeye laughed. "You don't catch me with that old trick," he snarled. "Now hand over the treasure."

The crocodile's mouth opened wider.

"There's a crocodile behind you!" yelled Captain Hailstone.

"Pull the other leg," growled Captain Deadeye.

And just at that moment
the crocodile's teeth snapped shut
round his legs. Before he could shout
"Shiver me timbers!" the crocodile
dragged him into the river. The pirates
watched dumbstruck as the bubbles
closed over their captain's head.

"I'm glad we didn't go for a swim first,"
said Pirate Windrush.

"He didn't get his treasure after all,"
said Pirate Redshanks.

"What treasure?" said Captain Hailstone.

"The treasure you're holding," said Pirate Redshanks.

Captain Hailstone held out his hand. "This isn't treasure," he said. "It's a very rare dinosaur fossil I wanted for my collection. I've been searching for it for years."

"But it says on this map that there's treasure here," said Pirate Greenhorn.

Captain Hailstone looked at the map and mopped his brow. "Well bless my soul!" he cried. "There's real treasure hidden right by the spot where we were digging. And to think we might have missed it!"

There was, too. A whole chest of it. Enough to send Captain Hailstone all round the world in search of other rare stones for his collection. Captain Deadeye's pirates decided to team up with him, and they sailed off together into the sunset.

The last light of day fell across Captain Hailstone's face as he smiled his toothy smile while Peanuts nibbled his ear.

"Who'd have thought we'd find the rare fossil I wanted *and* a chest full of treasure?"

"*You never know your luck!*" squawked Peanuts.

CAPTAIN KID

by Chris Powling

Shush!

Yes, *shush...*

That's how quiet it was on the *Golden Pegleg*, the second-biggest, second-boldest and second-baddest pirate ship that's ever sailed the Spanish Main.

"Shush!" said the First Mate to the Cabin Boy.

"Shush!" said the Bosun to the Cook.

"Shush!" said the Steersman to the Carpenter when he tried to whistle while he worked.

Even the Jolly Roger, as it flapped on the topmost mast, seemed to be shushing the pirates below. For days now, everyone on board had crept about on tiptoe with a finger pressed to their lips. "Shush!" they hissed. "Kindly shush - it's the Captain's orders."

Why was this?

Well, yesterday they'd come across a baby girl cast adrift in a rowing boat and Captain Forkbeard had gone all broody. "She's an omen, maties!" he told them. "She'll bring us good luck, I promise - provided we look after her properly."

"But we're pirates, Captain," protested the First Mate. "Pirates can't look after babies."

Forkbeard screwed up his face into his most horrible, terrible smile. "My pirates can," he growled. "Any man-jack here who upsets this baby had better be ready to upset *me*."

Naturally, that settled the matter. Mind you, the crew didn't like it.

It's hard to be a serious buccaneer when you can only say 'yo-ho-ho' in a whisper. And how do you fire a canon silently?

"Besides," the Steersman grumbled, "we've turned all our signal flags into nappies. What will the Captain do next, I wonder? Empty all the grog into the sea so he can use the jugs for feeding bottles?"

"I'm just about to do that," said the cook.

"What?"

"Forkbeard gave me the order this morning - I've got till nightfall to finish the job."

This was the last straw, of course.

So the pirates organized a mutiny. They sharpened their daggers, loaded their flintlock pistols and swished their cutlasses about in the air. Then they all went down below to the Captain's cabin.

For once they took Forkbeard by surprise. He'd been busy playing peep-bo with the baby. "You're not sea-dogs, you're sea-*rats*!" he roared as they tied him up. "How can you be so cruel to a little kid?"

"Just watch us, Captain," they answered. But it turned out there was nothing to watch.

After all, everyone knows the best way for a pirate to get rid of an unwanted shipmate.

"How can a baby walk the plank, though?" frowned the Bosun. "This kid's so little, it can't even *crawl* the plank."

"Goo-goo-goo," said the baby.

"We can't even clap her in irons," the Cabin Boy pointed out. "They'll never fit such a titchy kid."

"Oggy-oggy-oggy," the baby said.

After this, they talked about marooning her, or keel-hauling her or putting her back in the rowing boat and casting her adrift.

"Dad-a, Dad-a, Dad-a," crooned the baby as she gave the pirates a twinkly, dimply grin.

So that was the end of those suggestions.

Instead, they came up with an in-between idea which didn't seem *too* nasty but still let them feel a bit pirate-ish.

"Fix her a crib in the crow's-nest," they told the Carpenter.

"She'll be out of our way up there."

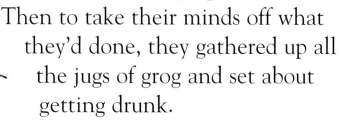

Then to take their minds off what they'd done, they gathered up all the jugs of grog and set about getting drunk.

"Yo-ho-ho!" came their shouts from below.

"Goo-goo-goo," came a tiny voice from above.

By the time night fell, and a thick, swirly mist covered the sea all round them, the pirates were fast asleep. It wasn't a happy sleep, though:

Hush-a-bye baby on the mast top,
When the wind blows the crow's-nest will rock,
When the mast breaks the crow's-nest will fall...

... and, in their pirate dreams, down came the baby, crow's-nest and all.

Maybe that's why they woke up at once when the whimpering began. It was faint, at first, and eerie - like a tingle up your spine. Soon it grew to a high-pitched howl which set your teeth on edge. Finally, deafeningly, it became a swooping, jaggedy screech that was enough to curdle your blood. And it went on and on and on...

The pirates stumbled up on deck. "It's that kid," they swore, "that dang-blasted kid!"

Then they saw why the baby was screaming.

Instantly, the whole crew took cover.

There, looming out of the midnight mist, was another pirate-ship - but not just any other pirate ship. This was the *Golden Hookhand*, not second-best like themselves, but the biggest, boldest, baddest pirate ship of them all.

"It's Captain Firebeard," gasped the Bosun. "He's Captain Forkbeard's mortal enemy! He'll sink us as soon as sneer at us. Say your prayers, maties. We're done for!"

"No we're not," said the Cabin Boy in surprise. "Look, they're giving up already!"

He was right.

With a frantic hauling on ropes and a panic-stricken spinning of the wheel, the *Golden Hookhand* was in full retreat.

"Steady as she goes, my hearties," yelled Captain Firebeard. "There's no shame in steering clear of a ghost ship! Nobody can beat a ghost ship!"

"Waa-Waa-Waa-Waa-Waaaaaaaa...!"

Magnified by the mist, the wail from the crib in the crow's nest was so shrill and spooky it could have come straight from Davy Jones's locker.

No wonder Firebeard was fleeing.

And no wonder the crew of the *Golden Pegleg* had to untie Captain Forkbeard a little later. Only he could stop the baby crying, you see.

Of course, he paid them out for the mutiny.

"Every last man-jack is on ship-scrubbing duty till further notice," he snarled. "Those of you who aren't on bottle-feeding, nappy-washing and cradle-rocking duty, that is. Now, *shush -* the whole lot of you."

And he went back to playing peep-bo with Captain Kid.

SQUEEZER AND THE SHIPTAKER

by Ian Whybrow

Pip and his cat Squeezer were on a mission, searching for a pirate ship. At last they stumbled upon a hidden Cornish harbour. And there she was - *The Seaslug*. Out came Pip's little mirror to catch the sun, and flash, flash, flash went his signal. Far out on the horizon, on the deck of a ship that looked no bigger than a bobbing gull, somebody saw and smiled.

Pip and Squeezer came to the busy dock and watched the men loading. Suddenly, there was a rumbling, thundering sound.

"Look out!" cried Pip. Squeezer just managed to jump from the cobbles up onto Pip's shoulder. A second later and he would have been squashed flat by a barrel of salted herring! The two sweaty sailors who had rolled it just laughed as if nothing had happened.

"That'll teach you to get in the way!" came a rough voice from above them.

A wicked-looking man with a beard grinned down at them from the deck. His face was red and his teeth were rotten. Even without his velvet cloak, there was no mistaking Mad Dan Wormwood, the most wanted pirate captain in England.

"Sling yer hook!" he cried.

Pip made no move to go.

Squeezer hissed and spat.

"Mister Mate!" roared Captain Wormwood. A great brute in a squashed hat appeared and dashed down the gangplank. From his broad belt, he pulled a pistol with six barrels. "Let's see you dance the Sailor's Hornpipe!" he snarled. BANG BANG! ZING ZING! Musket balls struck sparks off the cobbles by Pip's feet. Still Pip refused to move.

Wormwood slapped the ship's rail. "Hold yer fire, Mister Mate!" he called. "Bring that saucy young splinter aboard. I'll soon teach him some manners!"

A moment later, Pip was on board the pirate ship. He tried not to mind Mad Dan's horrible breath and to speak up bravely. "We'd like to join you, Captain," he said.

"What!!!" yelled Wormwood. "What use is a weedy boy and a stupid cat? Take that!" He whacked the seat of Pip's pants with the flat of his cutlass. It stung like mad but Pip did his best not to show it.

"I'll tell you what use we are," said Pip. "We capture ships."

Mad Dan Wormwood's hard hand grabbed the boy's yellow pigtail. "I ought to make you walk the plank, telling me lies like that!" he growled. Pip's eyes watered but he didn't cry. At last, Mad Dan let him go. "Well, Master Pip-squeak, you shall serve me as my Cabin Boy. And I'll promise you this: the day you take a ship, I'll bake me best britches and eat 'em, buttons and all!"

"Har har!" laughed the Mate. "The boy's a fool."

"Now get below, Mister Pip the Shiptaker!" ordered Mad Dan Wormwood. "There's spuds to peel and lavs to scrub. So look lively. We sail on the midnight tide."

And so they did. They slid silently out of the harbour on the twelfth stroke of the church clock. A mile from shore, Pip heard a cheer. The crew were lowering the Union Jack. Up in its place they hoisted... the skull-and-crossbones!

Pip's work was hard and filthy but he did not complain. All day, while the ship rolled and groaned, the boy was made to work like a slave. Pegleg the Bosun had him running everywhere. O'Keefe the Sailmaker loved to spit tobacco juice on deck and make him mop it up.

Wherever he went, the pirates teased him, tugged at his pigtail and aimed kicks at his backside. At night, he lay tired out and cold in his hammock. His only comfort was Squeezer, who curled round his head like a fur cap.

"We must learn to be patient and take a few knocks in this job!" whispered Pip.

By running errands all over the ship, Pip came to know every nook and cranny. And little Squeezer's yellow eyes were always sharp. Soon he knew the hiding place of every rat on board. But he never pounced. Like his young master, he was waiting for the right moment.

79

On the twenty-first day at sea, the Lookout gave a call from the crow's-nest.

"Sail-ho. Cargo ship on the starboard bow! Creeping along, too!"

"Easy pickings!" cried Mad Dan Wormwood. "All hands on deck! Man the guns! Stand by to take prisoners!"

Pip waited until every man was on deck ready for action. In the excitement, he was completely forgotten. It was the perfect time to carry out his secret plan.

"Right, Squeezer, do your duty. For England!"

Squeezer arched his back. His fur crackled with sparks, his claws shone like knives. Down he darted, into the dark places he knew so well, spitting and howling like a little devil. The rats leapt from their hiding places and squealed with terror as they fled. It was a stampede! They hopped over one another in their fright.

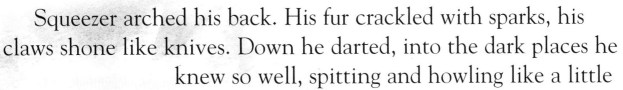

At the same time, Pip was down in the galley lighting the fuse to a small keg of gunpowder. As soon as it started to fizz, he popped it into the stewpot. "Three minutes!" he panted. "Let's hope Squeezer has done his work by now!"

Excited pirates were busy everywhere, so it took the boy two minutes to push his way to Mad Dan Wormwood's side by the ship's wheel. At that moment, the cargo ship opened fire with her one small canon.

"A popgun!" cried Wormwood. "She'll never even reach us!" The pirates cheered and booed, waving their cutlasses and letting off their pistols. At that moment, there was an ear-splitting boom.

"Oh no! A lucky shot! They've hit the gunpowder store, Captain!" yelled Pip. It was then that the pirate crew saw the rats streaming overboard like a waterfall.

"Look! The rats are leaving! We must be sinking like a stone!" they howled.

"Jump for it!" screamed the Mate. "Every man for himself!"

Coughing and spluttering in the cold water, Captain Wormwood clutched at a barrel for dear life. Imagine how surprised he was to look up and see that the *Seaslug* was still afloat. He was even more surprised to see a small boy with a yellow pigtail smiling down at him, and stroking a skinny cat.

"Jump, yer fool, the ship's going down!" yelled Mad Dan.

"I don't think so, Captain," Pip called. "My little bomb blew stew all over the galley, but otherwise there's no damage at all. Now please excuse us. Squeezer and I are expecting a visit from the Royal Navy very soon. We must go below and get things shipshape."

"You mean the ship with the popgun is a Navy vessel?" wailed the most wanted pirate captain in England.

"I'm afraid so, Captain," laughed Pip. "As soon as I found you, I signalled her to stand by for action. We knew you'd be looking for ships to rob in these waters! So you'll all be in irons before nightfall. What a pity you didn't believe that a weedy boy and a stupid cat could possibly capture a ship. Still, at least you'll have an interesting meal tonight."

"What are you talking about, you young dog?" wailed Mad Dan.

"Why, there's baked britches with button sauce for supper, I believe," grinned Pip the Shiptaker.

IN THE SOUP
by Tony Ramsay

Captain Melvin Mandrake, master of the bad ship *Blackheart* (and Terror of the Seas), had a daughter called Melody. Melody was quick and clever and determined to be a pirate like her father. She knew all there was to know about Swashing and Buckling and already could manage sixty-five of the Secret Seafarer's Knots all pirates know how to tie.

"Today's lesson," said Captain Mandrake one morning as they cruised the warm blue waters off Tristan da Cunha, "will be the Care and Training of Parrots..."

He had just begun a description of the seven different kinds of nautical parrot when a cry went up in the bows.

"All hands on deck! Mermaid in the nets!"

The lesson forgotten, Melody dropped her books and hurried forward. She arrived just in time to see the creature hauled onto the *Blackheart's* deck in a shower of silvery scales.

She had never seen a mermaid close up before. This one had skin like a smooth pink peach, a froth of golden curls and a fishy tail that smelt of the sea. Melody didn't like the look of her at all.

"You'd better put her back," she said. "It's bad luck to catch mermaids."

"Nonsense!" cried Captain Mandrake (The Terror of the Seas). "Why, look at her - she wouldn't harm a haddock!"

At this the mermaid fluttered her eyelashes and smiled a pink and watery smile. Then, to everyone's surprise, she started to sing. At once a dreamy look came over the *Blackheart's* crew. Every man-jack of them sank into a daze. Even bold Captain Mandrake (The Terror of the Seas) stretched out in his hammock with a smile.

When night fell, the pirates still hadn't moved.

"That was delightful," said Melody at last. "But isn't it time you were leaving?"

"Oh, I'm not leaving," said the mermaid lazily. "I like it here. I'm going to stay."

"Of course you must stay!" cried Captain Mandrake. "You can have my cabin. Melody will look after you. Now please - sing again!"

And the mermaid sang. Poor Melody didn't have a moment to herself. All day long she fetched and carried, and combed the mermaid's hair. And in the evening she filled the copper bath in the Captain's cabin so the mermaid could sing in the soapy water.

All this time, the crew of the *Blackheart* lay in their hammocks. They were so bewitched by the mermaid's singing they didn't stir for a week. They even stopped eating.

When she saw how thin the pirates were getting, Melody went straight to the mermaid. "The pirates are starving," she said. "If you don't stop this singing they'll fade away."

But the mermaid just laughed her watery laugh. "Foolish child," she said. "You're wasting your time. The ship is drifting. The first storm will sink her. They'll soon be fish food."

"Right," said Melody storming from the cabin. "Enough is enough!" And she climbed into the crow's-nest high above the deck and didn't come down till she'd thought of a plan.

That evening, she prepared the mermaid's bath as usual.

"The water's rather hot, isn't it?" said the mermaid.

"A little," said Melody. "But the steam is very good for your hair."

"Why, how splendid!" said the mermaid, wiping her golden mirror. "I have such lovely hair, you know."

When the bath was full to the brim, Melody added some onions.

"Onions?" said the mermaid. "What are those for?"

"Onions are very good for the complexion," said Melody. "Your skin will be smooth as silk."

"Will it really?" said the mermaid. "And the garlic?"

"For your scales," said Melody, dropping in the white cloves. "Garlic makes them strong and shiny."

The mermaid was delighted when Melody explained how good the herbs would be for her teeth and how important the slices of lemon were for keeping the eyes bright and clear.

"As for the salt and pepper," she added, sprinkling the silver pots into the bubbling water, "they'll make you sing better than ever."

"My, you are a clever girl," said the mermaid with a smile. "What a shame you'll soon be at the bottom of the sea."

When everything was ready, Melody left the mermaid to her bath.

Quite soon a mouth-watering smell started to seep under the cabin door. It crept along the *Blackheart*'s deck and down the companion-ways to where the pirates lay dozing. In his hammock, Captain Mandrake felt his moustache begin to twitch. There was something familiar about the smell. Something wonderful and delicious. Something even more powerful than a mermaid's magic.

"By thunder!" he cried, jumping to his feet. "I'm as hungry as a hump-backed whale!"

The others must have smelt it too. Because at that very moment pirates began to pour from every hatch and gangway - tall pirates, short pirates, pirates with earrings, pirates with pony tails, pirates of every shape and size. And each one of them carried a spoon.

No sooner had the stream of hungry pirates stormed into the captain's cabin than the mermaid - wet, bedraggled and smelling of onions - flopped through an open porthole and onto the deck.

"Those pirates are monsters!" she screeched. "I might have been eaten alive!"

Melody smiled sweetly. "They are rather hungry," she said, as they listened to the shouting and splashing and dipping of spoons. "I expect they'll be ready for the main course soon."

"Main course!" cried the mermaid. "If you think I'm staying here to be a pirate's dinner you are very much mistaken."

And with that she slithered across the deck, flicked her fishy tail and vanished over the side.

The last Melody saw of her was a single onion tangled in a stream of golden hair as she dived into the blue depths.

The extraordinary thing was, the pirates could remember nothing of what had happened. The whole adventure seemed to have vanished from their memory.

"Nonsense," said Captain Mandrake the next morning when Melody tried to explain. "You're making it up. Now look sharp! It's time for your lessons."

And he talked for an hour and a half about The Training of Parrots.

Melody didn't mind. Captain Mandrake may have forgotten the mermaid, but there was one thing she was sure he'd remember long after she'd learned all there was to learn about parrots.

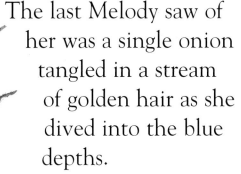

"I don't know what you put in it," he would say whenever they talked about Tristan da Cunha, "but that was the best fish soup I've ever tasted in my life!"